RUDOLPH
THE
RED-NOSED REINDEER®

Retold by Dennis R. Shealy
Illustrated by Linda Karl

A Random House PICTUREBACK® Book
Random House 🏠 New York

© 2004 The Rudolph Company, L.P. Under license to Character Arts LLC. All rights reserved. Published in the United States by Random House Children's Books, a division of Random House, Inc., New York, and in Canada by Random House of Canada Limited, Toronto. Rudolph the Red-Nosed Reindeer © & ® The Rudolph Co., L.P. Pictureback, Random House, and the Random House colophon are registered trademarks of Random House, Inc.　　　Library of Congress Control Number: 2002111767

ISBN: 978-0-375-82530-9
www.randomhouse.com/kids
Printed in the United States of America
13 12 11 10 9 8 7 6

Way, way up at the cold, cold North Pole,
there is a magical place called Christmastown.
Santa and his elves work here all year round,
making toys for good girls and boys.

And one night not so long ago,
something marvelous happened. . . .

A reindeer named Rudolph was born. But he wasn't like the other reindeer. He was . . . a little different.

Rudolph's parents were very concerned. "No son of
mine is going to have a nose that glows," declared his
father, Donner. Then he put a fake nose on Rudolph.

So Rudolph wore the fake nose, and he went out to play reindeer games with the other bucks every day. He had to, if he wanted to pull Santa's sleigh one day like his father. But Rudolph wasn't very happy.

Then one day he met a pretty doe named Clarice.
She whispered to him, "I think you're cute." Rudolph was
so excited, he started flying through the air!

When Rudolph landed, all the reindeer cheered. "Fantastic!" the coach yelled.

Rudolph finally felt as if he belonged. But then . . .

. . . his fake nose fell off!
   Everyone laughed when they saw his bright red nose.
Then someone called him Rudolph the Red-Nosed Reindeer,
and they laughed even more.

Rudolph was so embarrassed that he ran away.
He decided he was never, ever going back to
Christmastown. He just didn't belong.

And at the same moment, an elf named Hermey was running away from Christmastown, too. Hermey didn't want to make toys like the other elves. He wanted to be a dentist.

Rudolph and Hermey soon met and quickly became
friends. They decided to stick together, since it was
dangerous out there at the North Pole—especially
because of the Abominable Snow Monster.

The large, hungry creature could easily gobble up both of them in one bite. And Rudolph's glowing nose made it easy for the Abominable Snow Monster to follow them wherever they went.

The Abominable Snow Monster was chasing Rudolph and Hermey when they ran into a prospector named Yukon Cornelius. The prospector chipped off a large block of ice, and they all floated away from the fierce monster.

The ice took the new friends to the Island of Misfit Toys.
There they met a Charlie-In-The-Box, a polka-dotted elephant,
a train with square wheels, and many other toys that were
just a little different. The toys were sad because they thought
no one wanted to play with them.

The misfit toys took Rudolph and his friends to see their king, Moon Racer. The king explained to Rudolph that a toy that is not played with is not a toy at all. The toys on this island only wanted a boy or girl to love. Moon Racer hoped that Rudolph would ask Santa to find homes for them.

Rudolph agreed to tell Santa about the misfit toys.
That night Rudolph decided to return to Christmastown
alone. He knew the Abominable Snow Monster was still out
there, and he did not want his bright red nose to put
his friends in danger.

Back in Christmastown, Rudolph learned that his parents
and Clarice had gone to look for him and had never
returned. He knew exactly where to find them . . .

. . . in the cave of the Abominable Snow Monster! Rudolph
arrived just in time to save Clarice—but he was no match
for the gigantic beast.

Luckily, Yukon Cornelius and Hermey had followed Rudolph's trail to the cave. They had a plan to rescue their friend. Hermey lured the monster outside—and Cornelius dropped a big rock right on his head!

Safe at last, Rudolph and his friends returned to Christmastown. In all the excitement, everyone had forgotten that it was Christmas Eve. But once home, they learned that a terrible storm had forced Santa to cancel Christmas!

"But Santa, what about the good girls and boys?" Rudolph cried, his nose glowing brighter. "What about the misfit toys who need homes?"

"I'm sorry," Santa said, shielding his eyes. "The weather is just too bad to . . . Rudolph! Your wonderful nose! It's so bright! Why, you could guide my sleigh tonight!"
Christmas was saved!

Rudolph guided Santa's sleigh that night . . . and every Christmas after that. And he went down in history as the most famous reindeer of all—Rudolph the Red-Nosed Reindeer.